ASTRID & APOLLO

AND THE
HAPPY NEW YEAR

BY
V.T. BIDANIA

ILLUSTRATED BY
DARA LASHIA LEE

PICTURE WINDOW BOOKS
a capstone imprint

For my sister Sheng — V.T.B.

Astrid and Apollo is published by Picture Window Books,
an imprint of Capstone.
1710 Roe Crest Drive
North Mankato, Minnesota 56003
www.capstonepub.com

Library of Congress Cataloging-in-Publication Data

Names: Bidania, V. T., author. | Lee, Dara Lashia, illustrator.
Title: Astrid and Apollo and the happy New Year / by V. T. Bidania ;
   illustrated by Dara Lashia Lee.
Description: North Mankato, Minnesota : Picture Window Books, a Capstone
   imprint, [2020] | Series: Astrid and Apollo | Audience: Ages 6-8. |
   Summary: Astrid and Apollo are attending the Hmong New Year Festival
   (which is held at a big arena in Minneapolis or St. Paul in November or
   December), but in the crowded arena they are soon separated from their
   parents and younger sister, and between rescuing a little lost boy and
   getting mistaken for a pair of famous child singers, the festival turns
   into quite an adventure for the twins.
Identifiers: LCCN 2019058199 (print) | LCCN 2019058200 (ebook) |
   ISBN 9781515861256 (hardcover) | ISBN 9781515861294 (paperback) |
   ISBN 9781515861300 (adobe pdf)
Subjects: LCSH: Hmong American children—Juvenile fiction. |
   Hmong American families—Juvenile fiction. | Twins—Juvenile fiction. |
   Brothers and sisters—Juvenile fiction. | Hmong New Year—Juvenile fiction. |
   Ethnic festivals—Juvenile fiction. | CYAC: Hmong Americans—Fiction. |
   Twins—Fiction. | Brothers and sisters—Fiction. | Hmong New
   Year—Fiction. | Lost children—Fiction. | Festivals—Fiction.
Classification: LCC PZ7.1.B5333 An 2020 (print) | LCC PZ7.1.B5333 (ebook)
   | DDC [Fic]—dc23
LC record available at https://lccn.loc.gov/2019058199
LC ebook record available at https://lccn.loc.gov/2019058200

Additional coloring and artwork by Evelt Yanait.
Design Elements: Shutterstock: Ingo Menhard, Macrovector, Rusli, Yangxiong

Designer: Lori Bye

Printed and bound in the United States of America.
3342

Table of Contents

Hi, I'm Astrid. My twin brother is Apollo, and we were born in Minnesota. We live here with our mom, dad, and little sister, Eliana.

ASTRID GAO NOU

Hi, I'm Apollo! Our mom and dad were both born in Laos. They came to the United States when they were very young and grew up here.

APOLLO NOU KOU

MOM, DAD, AND ELIANA GAO CHEE

HMONG WORDS

gao (GOW)—girl; it is often placed in front of a girl's name. Hmong spelling: *nkauj*

Gao Chee (GOW chee)—shiny girl. Hmong spelling: *Nkauj Ci*

Gao Nou (GOW new)—sun girl. Hmong spelling: *Nkauj Hnub*

Hmong (MONG)—a group of people who came to the U.S. from Laos. Many Hmong from Laos now live in Minnesota. Hmong spelling: *Hmoob*

Nou Kou (NEW koo)—star. Hmong spelling: *Hnub Qub*

pa dow (PA dah-oh)—needlework made of shapes like flowers, triangles, and swirls. Hmong spelling: *paj ntaub*

pong zong (PONG ZONG)—lost or to become lost. Hmong spelling: *poob zoo*

qeng (GEHNG)—an instrument made of wood and bamboo. Hmong spelling: *qeej*

tou (TOO)—boy or son; it is often placed in front of a boy's name. Hmong spelling: *tub*

Tou Mong Zong (TOO Mong Zong)—a name for a boy that means "good luck." Hmong spelling: *Tub Hmoov Zoo*

CHAPTER 1

Don't Get Lost

Mom leaned down to speak, but Astrid could not hear her over the noise.

"What, Mom?" Astrid asked.

The arena was so noisy!

Astrid, Apollo, and their family had just arrived at the Hmong New Year Festival. They were excited to be there, even with the loud sounds all around.

Music came from the stage. Crowds of people stood everywhere talking. Some of them were singing New Year songs.

As more people walked by, the coins on their New Year clothes made a ringing noise. It sounded like hundreds of tiny bells!

Mom spoke again, but Astrid still couldn't hear her.

"It's too loud in here!" Astrid said.

Apollo cupped his hands around his mouth. "Mom said, 'DON'T GET LOST!'" he shouted.

"Okay, Mom!" Astrid said.

"It's loud and very crowded too," said Dad.

Apollo nodded. "We can barely move!" he said.

A family tried to walk past them. Astrid stepped to the side. The family squeezed through.

Dad looked past the big crowd in front of them. He saw a row of seats by the stage. He said, "Let's sit near the stage. Eliana will not want to go up there." Dad pointed to the seats on the second level.

"That's too high," said Mom.

Dad was carrying Eliana.

Eliana tapped Dad's shoulder and pointed up. "Too, too high!" Eliana said.

Astrid looked up. The seats went to the top of the arena. "I don't want to sit up there either," she said.

Apollo laughed. "I do!" he said.

"Go, go!" said Eliana. She pulled Dad's shirt.

"Eliana says it's time to go," Dad said and looked at the stage seats.

"Yes, let's go sit. Follow me," said Mom.

Eliana reached for Mom. Dad passed Eliana to her.

Mom carried Eliana on her hip. "Stay close! We don't want to lose anyone here. It will be very hard to find each other," she said.

"Kids, don't fall behind. No getting lost!" Dad smiled at them.

Astrid and Apollo nodded. Astrid knew she didn't want to get lost at the festival. The arena was too big. There were too many people.

Dad followed Mom and Eliana. Astrid followed Dad. Apollo followed her.

They walked in a single-file line into the crowd.

All of a sudden, a group of people cut in front of Astrid. They walked in between her and Dad.

"So sorry! Excuse us!" one of them said.

Astrid stopped so they could pass by. She looked at Apollo. Apollo shrugged.

The group was made up of young men and young women. Gold glitter covered their New Year clothes.

"They have to be dancers," Astrid said.

"You're right! They're going to the stage," said Apollo.

The dancers rushed to the back of the stage. The beads and coins on their clothes moved from side to side. They made ringing sounds.

"Jingle bells," Apollo said to Astrid.

Astrid laughed. It was true. The coins did sound like jingling bells!

The dancers' clothes shined under the arena lights.

Astrid and Apollo wore special Hmong New Year clothes too. Astrid wore a silky black jacket and white skirt. Apollo wore a vest and black pants.

Mom had given them sashes and belts with coins. She sewed Hmong pa dow designs onto the belts.

Astrid touched the coins on her belt as the dancers continued to pass them. The coins jingled. She smiled.

"This is taking forever!" said Apollo.

Astrid looked up. "How many dancers are there?"

Apollo crossed his arms over his chest. He made a face. He pretended to tap his foot on the floor.

Astrid was about to laugh again when she heard someone crying. She turned around.

A little boy stood a few feet from her. He was all alone. Tears fell down his face.

"Oh no! I think that little boy is lost!" said Astrid.

CHAPTER 2

Hiccups

Astrid took a step toward the boy.

He reached for her hand.

"Are you okay? Are you lost?" she asked.

The boy started to walk away. He pulled Astrid with him.

"Astrid, where are you going?" asked Apollo.

"Look!" Astrid pointed at the boy.

"We're supposed to follow Mom and Dad," said Apollo.

The little boy didn't let go of Astrid.
He closed his eyes and opened his
mouth wide. "Mama!" he cried.

"Apollo, what do I do?" Astrid asked.

Apollo walked over. He leaned down and asked, "Where's your mommy and daddy?"

The boy cried louder.

Astrid and Apollo looked around. They didn't see anyone who seemed like they were trying to find him.

"Maybe his family walked off. Maybe they don't know he got left behind," said Apollo.

"We can't leave him here," Astrid said. "He's so little. He's probably the same age as Eliana. What if *she* got lost?"

"Mama!" the boy said again. This time he pulled on Apollo's hand. He raised his arms.

"He wants you to carry him," said Astrid.

Apollo turned back to look at the crowd. The dancers were still walking by. "I can't see Mom and Dad anymore."

"Mama! Mama!" the boy said.

"Can you carry him?" asked Astrid.

Apollo picked him up. The little boy stopped crying. He started to hiccup.

"Now what?" asked Apollo.

"We could take him to the stage. They can announce that he's lost," said Astrid.

Apollo looked at the stage. Dancers danced in the middle of the stage. The band played their instruments behind them. Performers lined up by the stage steps. A big screen showed the host waiting on the side of the stage.

"They could show him on the screen. Then his family could see him!" said Astrid.

The little boy hiccuped again. He poked Apollo's shoulder. He pointed away from the stage.

"That way?" asked Apollo.

The little boy pointed again.

"Is your mama over there?" Astrid asked.

The little boy said, "Mama."

"Maybe she is," said Apollo. He walked in the direction the boy had pointed. Astrid followed him.

The little boy kept pointing. Astrid and Apollo kept walking.

They walked past the doors that led up to the second level. They walked by booths selling food. They walked by other booths selling gifts.

The arena floor was filled with thousands of people.

Children ran everywhere. Teenagers laughed with their friends. Pretty girls and handsome boys smiled at each other. Families talked to other families.

Just then, a ball flew past Astrid and Apollo. It almost hit their heads! They jumped to the side. The boy wiggled in Apollo's arms and laughed.

A young girl ran up to them. She picked up the ball. "Sorry!" she said before running back to her friends.

Astrid and Apollo watched balls flying through the air. People were playing catch nearby. It was a Hmong New Year game. They stood in rows and threw balls back and forth.

Some of them threw bright tennis balls. Some threw black cloth balls. Others played catch with shiny, glittery balls.

Astrid saw round orange balls. "Are those oranges?" she asked.

"They're actually using fruit to play catch!" said Apollo.

One orange rolled past their feet.

Suddenly Apollo said, "Maybe he can help us!"

He pointed at a police officer.

"We can bring the boy to him. He can help him find his family," Apollo said.

Astrid was about to say yes when someone yelled, "Tou Mong Zong!"

CHAPTER 3

Pong Zong

Astrid and Apollo turned around. A tall boy hurried up to them.

"Where did you go?" he said to the little boy.

The little boy smiled. His shoulders shook from hiccups. He reached his arms out to the tall boy.

"Do you know him?" Apollo asked.

The tall boy took him from Apollo.

"Thanks for finding my little brother!" he said. "He ran off from my mom." The little boy wrapped his arms around the tall boy.

"He was really scared," said Astrid.

The tall boy nodded. "Tou Mong Zong always walks off. He gets lost all the time. His nickname is Tou Pong Zong," he said.

Astrid smiled. Apollo laughed. The little boy's Hmong name meant *good luck*. His nickname meant *to be lost*.

"Thank you again!" the tall boy said.

Astrid and Apollo watched him carry Tou Mong Zong away. He waved at them, still hiccuping.

"He's so sweet," said Astrid.

"Well, good for Tou Mong Zong. But now *we* are pong zong!" said Apollo.

Astrid put her hands on her hips. "Apollo Nou Kou Lee! We just helped a little boy. You should be glad!"

Apollo held up both hands. "Okay, but how will we find Mom and Dad now?" he asked.

"We go back to the spot from before, when we were behind them," said Astrid.

She tried to look for that spot. But she couldn't remember where it was.

"Which way is it?" asked Apollo. Everywhere he looked, everything looked the same.

"We were over there," said Astrid. She pointed to the doors near the entrance.

"That's far. We were closer to the stage," said Apollo.

Astrid looked around. She saw two stages! Each stage was on a different side of the arena. "Which stage?" she asked.

Apollo pointed to one stage. "I'm sure it was that one," he said. But he didn't sound like he was sure.

"Didn't we turn around? Maybe it's the other one," said Astrid.

Apollo scratched his head. "I don't know," he said.

Just as they turned around again, another orange flew past them.

"Watch out!" Astrid said.

They ducked. When they stood up, Apollo saw a woman walking by. She was holding a leash.

"A dog!" said Apollo.

The woman walked close to them. Her dog was big. It wore a red vest.

"That's a service dog. It helps people. We're not supposed to pet it," Astrid said.

"I just want to see what it looks like," said Apollo.

They took a closer look at the dog. It was a light cream color. It looked friendly. Its tail wagged as it walked away.

"That's a cool dog," said Apollo. "If we had one, I'd play fetch with it."

"I'd rather have a little dog," Astrid said. "Small dogs are so cute. We could still play fetch with it too!"

Another ball flew by. Astrid and Apollo moved back.

"Let's get away from the ball players," said Apollo.

They walked closer to the wall. Not as many people were there.

Astrid looked at the crowds. Could they find Mom and Dad in there? She took a deep breath. "Apollo, I'm sorry."

Apollo looked over at the stages again. "Don't worry," he said.

But the arena was so big. There were people everywhere. Apollo was starting to worry too.

"What if we go to one stage and check the seats? If they aren't there, we can go to the other stage," said Astrid.

Apollo nodded. "Let's do that."

"But what if they're not there because they're looking for us?" Astrid asked. She really did not want to be lost.

"If we can't find them, we'll go to the stage for help. They'll announce we're lost and everything will be okay," said Apollo.

Astrid bit her lip. "This is my fault," she said.

"But the little boy was scared. You helped him," Apollo said.

Astrid didn't say anything. Apollo could tell she felt bad.

"Let's go over there," he said.

"Where?" Astrid asked.

"I saw something you'll like!" said Apollo.

CHAPTER 4

Three Little Puppies

Astrid and Apollo walked past more people. They had to go around a group taking pictures. They passed people taking videos of the festival too.

Then they walked past the food section. Lines of people waited to buy food.

Apollo sniffed the air. "I can smell fried chicken," he said.

"Where are we going?" Astrid asked.

Apollo pointed to a row of booths selling gifts. "There!" he said.

Astrid's eyes lit up. "Cute!"

There was a booth selling flowers and balloons. Next to that was a booth with stuffed animals and toys. A big plastic box was full of little toy puppies.

Astrid hurried up to the box. She smiled at the stuffed toy puppies.

"I knew you'd like them," said Apollo. "They're not real, but they look real."

"I love them!" Astrid said. "I wish I had one. A real one."

"Would you like to see a puppy?" the woman behind the counter said.

Astrid turned to Apollo. "We're supposed to be looking for Mom and Dad."

"You can see it first," said Apollo.

Astrid nodded. The woman picked a puppy from the box. She handed it to Astrid.

Astrid knew it was only a toy, but she held the puppy like it was real. She petted the white fur.

"She's so soft," Astrid said.

Apollo laughed. "You look like you're holding a real puppy."

The woman smiled. "All toys in the plastic box are on sale," she said. "A little girl just bought three toy puppies. It was right before you came here."

"Three?" asked Astrid.

The woman nodded. "You can ask your mom and dad to buy it for you."

Astrid looked at Apollo. She really missed her parents now.

"Thank you," said Astrid. She handed back the toy puppy. "We'll come back later."

Astrid and Apollo walked away from the toys.

Astrid looked down. Glitter sparkled on the floor. It fell there from everyone's shiny New Year clothes.

"Don't worry, Astrid," said Apollo. "We'll find Mom and Dad, I promise."

* * *

Astrid and Apollo made their way to the middle of the arena. They were getting better at walking around people.

"We'll go to this stage first," said Apollo. "We'll check the seats for Mom and Dad."

"Okay," Astrid said. "If we don't see them, we'll go to the other stage."

They ran to the first stage. As they
got closer, they saw a man on the
stage holding a qeng. He blew into
the Hmong instrument and music
came out. It sounded like a loud hum.

As the man played the qeng, he
walked in small circles.

Astrid and Apollo stood by the seats and watched.

The man turned in the other direction. He walked in more circles. Then he leaned down and did a fast forward roll. He stood right back up and walked in a circle again.

Everyone clapped.

"He didn't stop playing the qeng!" said Astrid.

"He rolled, and it stayed in his mouth!" said Apollo. "I bet I can do that."

"You're silly!" Astrid said, laughing.

When the man with the qeng was done, people clapped again.

Then a group of teenage boys got on the stage. They weren't wearing Hmong clothes like the man. They wore black jeans and black T-shirts. They stood with their arms crossed. When music played from the speakers, the boys began to break dance.

The audience cheered.

Two boys did handstands and spun on the floor. The other boys moved to the side. Then they came out and did flips across the stage.

Everyone shouted and clapped. Someone made a loud whistling sound.

Astrid and Apollo smiled.

"Are you going to say you can do that too?" Astrid teased Apollo.

Apollo grinned and said, "No, that's too easy."

Astrid shook her head and laughed.

When the dance was done, the host spoke into a microphone. It squealed loudly.

Astrid and Apollo covered their ears.

"Let's look for Mom and Dad now!" said Apollo.

"You check the seats on the left. I'll check on the right," said Astrid.

Astrid and Apollo walked up and down the aisle. All the seats were taken. Some people were standing up. It was hard to see every seat. They had to peek in between the people who were standing.

They saw babies in strollers, grandparents talking to each other, and families eating food at their seats. They saw people smiling about the performers or talking on their phones. They even saw a tired man sleeping on a chair. But they did not see Mom and Dad and Eliana.

"They're not here," said Astrid. "I looked at each row three times."

"Me too," said Apollo. "Should we go to the next stage?"

"Yes. If they're not there, we have to talk to the host. They have to announce we're lost," said Astrid. She was feeling nervous about that too.

"I hope we find them first," said Apollo. "I don't want to go up on the stage."

Astrid shook her head. "Me neither."

When they got to the other stage, they saw a group of teenage girls. They were wearing fancy dresses. The girls were carefully walking down the stage steps.

"They're from the pageant! That's why they have pretty dresses. The one with the best walk and best dress wins. She gets to be Miss Hmong!" said Astrid.

One of them carried red roses. She had a shining crown on her head.

"That must be the winner," said Apollo.

Astrid smiled. "She's beautiful!"

The teenage girls walked away in a long line.

Astrid and Apollo were standing near the steps when the host saw them. She waved and said, "Come on!"

CHAPTER 5

You're Famous!

"Us?" said Apollo.

The host nodded and came down to them. "Hurry!" she said. She took Astrid's hand and led her to the stage.

Astrid turned to look at Apollo. She was confused.

Apollo followed her. He was confused too.

"We were waiting for you!" the host said.

"You were?" Astrid asked.

"Of course!" she said.

"How did you know?" asked Apollo. They were now standing on the stage. Bright lights hung above them.

The host laughed. "Everyone knows about you! Watch the cords," she said. She pointed at the black cords coming from the speakers.

"But how?" Astrid asked.

"You're famous!" she said.

Astrid and Apollo looked at each other in surprise.

The host gave them two small microphones. "You can wear these. I'll help you put them on your shirts."

"Why do we need them?" asked Apollo.

"So people can hear you!" she said. She put the first one on Astrid's jacket.

"We have to talk?" said Astrid. She looked out at the seats. So many people would see and hear them. She was getting more nervous.

The host laughed again. She stuck the other microphone on Apollo's shirt.

"Can you talk for us?" asked Apollo. He was starting to feel very shy.

The host didn't answer his question. "Make sure you are loud. Remember to look at the camera." She pointed to a big camera at the front of the stage.

"What do we say?" Apollo said. "Just our names? Do we say our parents' names?"

She clapped her hands together. "How nice! It's always good to mention your parents. You can thank them!"

Astrid didn't understand. "Why would we thank our mom and dad?" she asked.

The host made a face. "Well, you don't have to, then. Just say, 'Happy New Year! Happy New Year!' Like that." She waved her arms in the air.

"What?" Astrid whispered to Apollo.

The host said, "When you're ready, we'll start the music. Then you start singing." She quickly walked away.

Astrid stared at Apollo.

"She thinks we're someone else! We have to go!" said Astrid.

Apollo unhooked his microphone. As Astrid took hers off, the host came back.

"What are you doing?" she said. "We're behind schedule!"

"We aren't singing!" said Astrid. She gave her the microphone.

"You can't leave! Your song is about to start. You're on camera. See?" she said.

Astrid and Apollo turned to the screen. They saw themselves up close. People in the audience were watching them and talking. Everyone seemed confused too.

"We're not singers. We're just lost. We want our mom and dad!" said Astrid. Her lips were shaking. She was trying hard not to cry.

Apollo's cheeks turned red. "I'm sorry. Can you please tell our parents to come get us?"

Just as he said that, Apollo heard someone yelling their names. He and Astrid looked toward the edge of the stage.

Eliana was sitting on Dad's shoulders. She held a toy puppy. She screamed, "Astrid! Apollo!"

* * *

Astrid and Apollo were back with Mom, Dad, and Eliana. They were watching the show. Mom was fixing Astrid's hair. Apollo was playing with Eliana and her three toy puppies.

Dad smiled at them. "Astrid and Apollo, you surprised us up there. I'm glad we found each other."

"We are too," said Astrid. She was so happy to be with her parents and Eliana again. "From now on, we're going to stay close to you always."

"I like that," said Mom.

Astrid hugged her tight.

"Next time, ask an adult for help right away," Mom said.

Astrid and Apollo nodded. "Okay," they said.

"I promise we'll never get lost again!" said Apollo.

"It's a deal," said Dad. He shook Apollo's hand and messed up his hair.

Suddenly, the audience clapped. Astrid and Apollo looked up at the stage.

A young boy and girl were up there with small microphones attached to their clothes. Music played. Just before they sang, they waved their arms in the air and said, "Happy New Year! Happy New Year!"

Everyone cheered, and Astrid and Apollo laughed.

FACTS ABOUT THE HMONG

- Hmong people first lived in southern China. Many of them moved to Southeast Asia in the 1800s. Some Hmong decided to stay in the country of Laos (pronounced LAH-ohs).

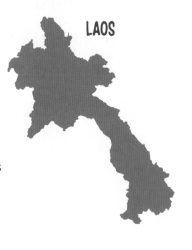

LAOS

- In the 1950s, a war called the Vietnam War started in Southeast Asia. The United States joined this war. They asked the Hmong in Laos to help them. When the U.S. lost the war, Hmong people had to leave Laos.

- After 1975, many Hmong came to the U.S. as refugees. Refugees are people who escape from their country to find a new, safe place to live. Today, Minnesota is home to around 85,000 Hmong.

MORE ABOUT
THE HMONG NEW YEAR

• The Hmong New Year Festival happens every November or December in Minnesota. It is held at a big arena in St. Paul or Minneapolis. People like to dress up in pretty Hmong New Year clothes to celebrate. At the festival, everyone can play catch, watch talent shows, eat good food, and do other activities. Hundreds of thousands of Hmong people from all over the world come to join the fun!

• Catch is a game played during the Hmong New Year. Players throw a ball back and forth and sometimes sing songs while they play. Balls can be made of solid black or shiny cloth. People use tennis balls to play too!

• Silver coins hang from beads on Hmong New Year clothes. The coins ring like bells when people walk. They are noisy and sparkly!

GLOSSARY

arena (uh-REE-nuh)—a large building that is used for sports or entertainment

break dance (BRAYK DANSS)—a kind of dancing in which a dancer does very athletic movements that involve touching the ground with parts of the body such as the head or back

design (di-ZINE)—a pattern

festival (FES-tuh-vuhl)—a party or holiday

hiccup (HIK-uhp)—to make a gulping sound caused by a sudden movement in your chest that you cannot control

pageant (PAJ-uhnt)—a contest in which a group of girls or women compete to show their talents and skills, their dresses, and the way they speak and look

performer (pur-FOR-mur)—a person who entertains an audience

sash (SASH)—a wide strip of material worn around the waist or over one shoulder as a decoration or part of a uniform

schedule (SKEJ-ul)—a plan of things that will be done and the times they will be done

TALK ABOUT IT

1. Why was the Hmong New Year Festival so noisy? Share a time when you went to a noisy event. Talk about the loud sounds you heard.

2. Astrid was worried when she and Apollo got lost at the New Year Festival. Have you ever gotten lost? Talk about what happened. If not, talk about a place where you do not want to get lost!

3. At the festival, people were playing catch, a fun Hmong New Year game. Discuss the kinds of balls they used to play.

WRITE ABOUT IT

1. Astrid and Apollo walked around the arena and saw many different people. Write a paragraph about who they saw and what activities they were doing.

2. When they went on the stage, Astrid and Apollo felt nervous. Write about a time you felt nervous or shy to be in front of a big group of people.

3. Astrid wants to get a pet puppy. Do you have a pet? If not, is there an animal you would like for a pet? Draw a picture of your pet or favorite animal. Write a sentence to describe it.

ABOUT THE AUTHOR

V.T. Bidania was born in Laos and grew up in St. Paul, Minnesota. She spent most of her childhood writing stories, and now that she's an adult, she is thrilled to be writing stories for children. She has an MFA in creative writing from The New School and is a recipient of the Loft Literary Center's Mirrors and Windows Fellowship. She lives outside of the Twin Cities with her family.

ABOUT THE ILLUSTRATOR

Dara Lashia Lee is a Hmong American illustrator based in the Twin Cities in Minnesota. She utilizes digital media to create semi-realistic illustrations ranging from Japanese anime to western cartoon styles. Her Hmong-inspired illustrations were displayed at the Qhia Dab Neeg (Storytelling) touring exhibit from 2015 to 2018. When she's not drawing, she likes to travel, take silly photos of her cat, and drink bubble tea.